Licensed exclusively to Top That Publishing Ltd
Tide Mill Way, Woodbridge, Suffolk, IP12 1AP, UK
www.topthatpublishing.com
Copyright © 2017 Tide Mill Media
All rights reserved
2 4 6 8 9 7 5 3 1
Manufactured in China

Written by Oakley Graham
Illustrated by Lizzie Walkley

ISBN 978-1-78700-050-6

A catalogue record for this book is available from the British Library

'For Clare, who shares and is always there. x OG'

# The Bear Who Would Not Share

Written by Oakley Graham

Illustrated by Lizzie Walkley

Bear had spent the whole morning baking cakes and had covered them in yummy icing.

They looked and smelled amazing!

Bear was admiring his cakes
when there was a loud knock
on his front door.

Knock,
knock!

'Hello Bear,' said Owl.
'I was flying by and I couldn't help but notice the delicious smell coming from your house.

I don't suppose that you would share one of your yummy cakes covered in icing with me?' said Owl, as he peered at the cakes in the kitchen.

'No!' said Bear.

As Bear started to clear up the mess that he had made whilst baking, there was a second knock on his front door.

'That's strange,' said Bear. 'I don't usually have many visitors.'

Bear opened the door and was surprised to see Fox on his doorstep.

'Hello Bear,' said Fox. 'I was walking by and I couldn't help but notice the delicious smell coming from your house.

I don't suppose that you would share one of your yummy cakes covered in icing with me?' said Fox, as she spied the cakes in the kitchen.

'No!'
said Bear.

Bear went back to cleaning the kitchen and
had almost finished when he heard the sound
of knocking on his front door again.

'Hello Bear,' said Rabbit.
'I was hopping by and I couldn't
help but notice the delicious smell
coming from your house.

I don't suppose that you would
share one of your yummy cakes
covered in icing with me?'
said Rabbit, as he admired
the cakes on display.

**'No!'**
said Bear.

News of Bear's yummy cakes covered in icing quickly spread throughout the neighbourhood and many of Bear's friends came to visit him ...

'No!'
'No!'
'No!'

After a busy morning of baking,
Bear was feeling very tired.
He stopped to admire his cakes once
more, then went upstairs to have a nap.

When Bear woke up from his nap he was very hungry indeed! He couldn't wait to eat one of his yummy cakes covered in icing.

But when he got downstairs,
Bear could not believe his eyes.

The yummy cakes covered
in icing were gone!

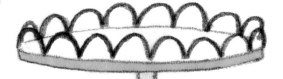

Bear raced outside ...

'Rabbit, have you seen my yummy cakes covered in icing?'

'Erm ... no!'

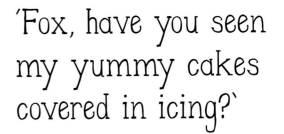

'Fox, have you seen my yummy cakes covered in icing?'

'Um ... no!'

'Owl, have you seen my yummy cakes covered in icing?'

'Er ... no!'

Then Bear saw his cub,
Little Bear, holding one of his
yummy cakes covered in icing.

Little Bear had seen the cakes
and had decided to share them
with his friends.

Although Little Bear should have asked if he could share the cakes, Bear could not be angry with him.

Seeing all of the happy faces covered in icing, Bear realised that it was good to share.

'I don't suppose that you would share some yummy cake covered in icing with me?' said Bear, as he admired the last cake Little Bear was holding.

'Yes!'

Little Bear replied.